Easter Joke Book for Kids

Try Not to Laugh Challenge

Interactive Easter Jokes Basket
Stuffer for Kids with Funny
Knock Knock Jokes, Silly Riddles
and Puns

Thank you for your purchase!

If you love this book, and you would like to see more like it, please leave a review.

Every review makes a huge difference!

First, a GAME...

Try Not to Laugh Spring Challenge!

Rules:

Pick your team, or go one by one. Each player has to tell one joke, making silly faces, funny sound effects, and so on.

If your opponent laughs, you will get a point.

First team to win 5 points, is the WINNER!

Jokes, Pun Jokes and Funny Riddles with Answers

Q: How do you call a thief caught steeling eggs?

A: Egg-sposed.

Q: Where does an Easter Bunny shop?

A: At the ONE HOP SHOP! (One stop shop)

Q: How do you call a happy egg?

A: Egg-cited.

Q: How does a rooster invite a hen to dance?

A: He tells her "Let's shake an egg!"

Funny tip – "Shake a leg" means "Let's dance!"

Q: How do you call the chicken's Paradise?

A: Hen-ven. (Heaven)

Q: How do you call an egg hatching on a plane?

A: Eggs-treme.

Q: How do you call a baby owl?

A: A Yell-ow!

Q: How do you call a chocolate egg?

A: Egg-special.

Q: How do you call a cat who swallowed a chicken?

A: Purr-poule.

Funny tip – "Poule" means "hen" in French.

Q: How do you know a rabbit's age?

A: Simple- all the grey hares are really old!

Q: Why does the Easter bunny love to give hugs?

A: Because it adores hoppy people! (Happy)

Q: Why is the Easter Bunny scared?

A: Because he's in a harey situation!
(Scary)

Q: Which bunny was sent to the doctor?

A: The Bugs Bunny.

Q: What did the Tooth Fairy speak about when she met the little bunny?

A: Her Fairy tail!

Q: What did the father bunny say to his son when he left for school?

A: Break an egg!

Funny tip – "Break a leg!" means "Good luck!"

Q: What do you name a Bunny Cooker?

A: Hop Chef! (Top Chef).

Q: What convinced the doe to marry the rabbit?

A: A 14-carrot gold necklace.

Funny tip – a doe is a rabbit female.

Q: Did you like my Valentine? Asked the rooster.

A: It was Egg-cellent! Said the hen.

Q: **What kind of food does the Easter Bunny love?**

A: Hop Dog! (Hot dog)

Q: What kind of plants does the hen love?

A: Egg-plants.

Q: Why did the rooster catch the thief?

A: Because he was no longer a chicken!

Q: Where does the Easter Bunny live?

A: On Carrot Earth!

Q: Why did the coach congratulate the players?

A: Because he saw hare play! (Fair play)

Q: How do you impress a modern bunny?

A: You email him a carrot!

Q: How do rabbits punish the bad guys?

A: They put them into the NO NEST AREA. (No rest area)

Q: Why did the Bunny enter the music contest?

A: Because he loved to play hip-hop!

Q: Where does the rabbit driver pull over the car?

A: In the nest area.

Funny Tip – The Rest Area on a motorway is an area where a driver can have some rest

Q: In what movies did the hen star in?

A: "Hen in black" and "Mad hen"!

Q: What do you call a super-hen?

A: X-hen!

Q: How did a bunny get a peacock tail?

A: He bought it at the re-tail store.

Q: Why did the roster send his wife to the gym?

A: Because he thought she needed to eggs-ercise!

Q: What sound does a chick's phone make?

A: Peep – peep!

Q: What does the rabbit family read?

A: The Easter's Digest!

Mommy: "Dear, what do you think you would like to be when you grow up?"

Girl: "The Easter bunny!"

Mommy "Why?"

Girl "Because he can have as many chocolate eggs as he likes!"

Q: What said the rabbit to his wife?

A: I am hoping to see you later!

Q: What says the worm to the chicken?

A: Scratch me if you can! (Catch me is you can)

Q: Why did the chicken student stay at home?

A: He was sick with people's pox.

Q: Why does the hen love it when she goes in the oven?

A: She knows she's going to be one hot chick!

Q: How do you call a hen that only laid one egg?

A: Egg-centered.

Funny tip – Egocentric is a person having little or no regard for interests, beliefs, or attitudes other than one's own.

Q: What kind of disk used mother rabbit to save her pictures?

A: A floppy disk.

Funny tip – A floppy disk was used to store data from a computer.

Q: How do rabbits travel in space?

A: They go through hoper-space!

Funny tip – Hyperspace is a faster-than-light (FTL) method of traveling used in science fiction.

Q: How does a hen know how many eggs are needed for Easter?

A: She doesn't know. She only egg-stimates. (Estimates)

Q: Why was the hen first in class at math?

A: She knew all the egg-uations. (Equation)

Q: Why did the chicken leave the farm?

A: He wanted to get some egg-ucation. (Education)

Q: **From what country comes the Easter Egg?**

A: From Egg-ypt.

Q: What kind of doctor did the Easter Bunny wanted to be?

A: A ort-hop-pedist. (Orthopedist)

Funny tip – An orthopedist is a doctor for your bones.

Q: Why did the Bunny enter the contest?

A: He was feeling hop-ful he could win!

Knock Knock Jokes and Funny Puns

Knock, knock!

Who's there?

Bun.

Bun who?

The Easter Bunny, I brought you some gifts!

Knock knock!

Who's there?

Egg.

Egg who?

I feel eggs-excellent!

Knock, knock!

Who's there?

Hare.

Hare who?

I need your hair dryer.

Knock knock!

Who's there?

Hen.

Hen who?

Honey, I feel funny!

Knock knock!

Who's there?

Hop.

Hop who?

I was hopping to see you!

Knock knock!

Who's there?

Ear.

Ear who?

I am erasing you!

Knock knock!

Who's there?

Chick.

Hop who?

Check your kitchen - it smells like smoke.

Knock knock!

Who's there?

Chick.

Hop who?

Check your kitchen – it's stinky!

Knock knock!

Who's there?

Ring.

Who rings?

Come out – spring is here!

Knock knock!

Who's there?

Hip.

Hip who?

Wanna dance hip-hop?

Knock knock!

Who's there?

Lilly.

Lilly who?

I bought a bunch of lilies.

Knock knock!

Who's there?

Treat.

What treat?

Let's retreat together in Madagascar!

Knock knock!

Who's there?

Duc.

Duc who?

Donald Duck!

Knock knock!

Who's there?

Ness.

Ness who?

I wanna nest here.

Knock knock!

Who's there?

Wm.

Wm who?

Quick! A hen wants to eat me.

Knock knock!

Who's there?

Son.

Son who?

Come out, It's so sunny!

Your Bunny (money) or your life!

Knock knock!

Who's there?

Nee.

Nee who?

Need to see you.

Knock knock!

Who's there?

Joy.

Joy who?

Joyful to see it's spring!

Knock knock!

Who's there?

Flo.

Flo who?

This flower is for you.

Knock knock!

Who's there?

Choo.

Choo who?

I've got chocolate and I'm not sharing!

Earning Bunny (money) for
nothing

Knock knock!

Who's there?

Hunt.

Hunt who?

Hunt chocolate eggs with me!

Milk and Bunny

(Honey)

Knock knock!

Who's there?

Joe.

Joe who?

Joe Mama.

Knock knock!

Who's there?

Abby.

Abby who?

About your birthday – I forgot your gift.

Knock knock!

Who's there?

Anna.

Anna who?

Another Easter Egg.

Knock knock

Who's there?

Wayne.

Wayne who?

Don't whine like a chicken.

A taste of Bunny (Honey)

Knock knock

Who's there?

Chicken.

Chicken who?

Check your head – I think you lost it.

Time is Bunny!
(Money)

Knock knock

Who's there?

Orange.

Orange who?

Are you going to eat that

chocolate egg?

Knock knock!

Who's there?

Anee.

Anne who?

Anne Easter Bunny.

Knock knock!

Who's there?

Henrietta.

Henrietta who?

Henrietta chicken in my yard.

Knock knock!

Who's there?

Fool.

Fool who?

Fooled you!

Bunny Valentine
(Funny)

Knock knock

Who's there?

Alaska.

Alaska who?

I'll ask the Easter Bunny to bring you more eggs!

Thank you for your purchase!

If you love this book, and you would like to see more like it, please leave a review.

Every review makes a huge difference!

Other Books for Kids:

Emilia's Treasure

How a mermaid makes friends

Anca Niculae
Illustrator Maria Falie

And there are more to come!

Printed in Poland
by Amazon Fulfillment
Poland Sp. z o.o., Wrocław